THE BLACK WIDOW

A PHILIPPINE MYTHOLOGY FANTASY

Mayumi Cruz

Romantic Suspense
THE BILLIONAIRE'S WIDOW

Romantic Comedy
IT'S NOT JUST SEMANTICS

Romantic Comedy Adventure
ESCAPE TO LOVE (Book 1, Meet the Petersons)
HUNTED HONEYMOON (Book 2, Meet the Petersons)

Women's Fiction
THE UNFAITHFUL WIFE

Children's Picture Book
RENZO'S RAINBOW

Journal
MY SMILE JOURNAL

CHAPTER 1

Black Encantada

The brilliant red, odd-looking shape was what my eyes caught first. With each movement, it stretched out gracefully, much like a yawning mouth. And then, just as slowly, I watched it deflate like a balloon, going back to its original form.

I frowned, searching my mind for what it reminded me of. But however hard I tried, it eluded me. I shook my head. My brain was not the same as before.

Fog, debilitating, had crept in.

The legs came into view next. I cocked my head to one side, squinting my eyes. The grotesque, gangly, stick-like figure was hypnotizing as it was confounding. They were disjointed; yet connected at the same time.

I counted.

One. Two. Three. Four. Five. Six. Seven.

Divided into seven segments. Joined together precariously like pieces of tacky clay. Each leg was covered in patches of uneven, thin hair; some long, some short.

Curved, combed bristles adorned each leg's bottom. Belatedly, I realized they were miniature feet.

Feet that were dragging themselves on the surface of my right hand. They treaded firmly, step by step, awakening my nerve endings, filling me with a mix of weird sensations.

At first, it felt like a light caress, feather-like. I closed my eyes, letting the feeling overwhelm me.

Gradually, it became somewhat ticklish, like tiptoeing to the beat of unheard music. I stifled a smile.

And then, all at once, it pricked my skin with the intensity of a long, sharp needle.

I snapped my eyes open. The hair on my arms raised alarmingly at the sight of hind legs kicking, flailing in the air. The rest of it was missing. It was *embedding* itself into my flesh.

Paralyzed, I watched with a mixture of horror and awe as it burrowed deeper, deeper until I could no longer see any part of it.

It was, fully, completely, *inside* me. I felt it crawling, biting, nibbling on my flesh, *devouring* me from inside.

Instinctively, I raised my left arm over my right hand, wanting to prevent the creature from further ingraining itself inside me.

To my horror, I saw my left hand.

Or rather, the *lack* of it.

In place of my left hand, an open, hideous wound met my sight. Freshly-dried blood and bright yellow green pus covered the cropped, swollen limb and tissues where my hand previously had been. Gangrene was already evident, the horrid, stomach-turning stench almost making me puke.

Elsewhere, the noises of the insects scouring the night were getting louder, more terrifying than any night before. The rustle of the tree branches echoed endlessly, singing an eerie, haunting tune.

My nose captured a familiar, lingering scent. The citrusy vanilla scent of a yet unnamed, undiscovered wild orchid scattered around our village, perched in tree limbs a few feet above the ground. It pervaded my nostrils. For a moment, my muddled mind wondered why I was smelling it inside my bedroom.

Flashes of memory persisted, bringing sparks of light to an otherwise dark room that was my mind. A humongous fallen tree trunk carved, transformed into a bathtub. Pile upon pile of wild orchid flowers thrown into warm bathwater. My naked body descending on the aromatic, erotic purple pool. My hand groping underwater for another kind of flower, a thousand times more intoxicating and infinitely more satisfying.

Where I lost myself completely for two days and two nights.

Where my raging libido was satisfied over and over and over again.

Where I buried my body and planted my precious seed.

Suddenly, I remembered what the odd-looking shape reminded me of.

It was the shape of a woman's body. An hourglass. The identifying mark of a poisonous black widow spider.

Regrets, alas, did always come too late. I should have listened to my mentor. The old folks were right.

My wife was a black encantada.

CHAPTER 2
The Mentor

I would stay away from her if I were you, Datu."

Malek wasn't one to mince words. Most times I appreciated him for that. Sometimes, I didn't. And this was one of those times.

My mentor and best friend was much, much older than me. He had been my father's trusted right-hand man, as well as my ancestors' before him.

Malek's clearly defined muscles bulging under his clothes bespoke of a strength that had been proven time and time again.

Withered hands and wrinkled face aside, his mind remained alert, headstrong. Thick, bushy silvery brows atop piercing black eyes and coffee-colored age spots on his face only added to his stern look of wisdom and experience.

He had seen through three generations of our family.

It was rare for him to visit me in my house. He preferred to stay in his home, passing away the time in a multitude of small chores like gardening, cleaning, and reading. After his wife and son died, he turned hermit, refusing to go out and mingle with the living, finding solace in memories of the distant happy past, of days that will never come back.

I ought to be thankful that he was compelled to come out of seclusion. Countless times in the past, I was the one who sought him out, asking for his well-meaning advice. Presently, however, his reprimand was not to my liking. His tone was downright condescending.

He may be my mentor, but I was still king of my domain.

Many, many years ago, he and my great grandfather, together with their families and closest friends, settled in this tiny patch of land, a clearing completely off the beaten track, deep inside a rainforest in Southern Mindanao. They could not have picked a better choice.

The forest was ancient, the kind where animals and birds may have roamed freely in the past, but had since lost its former glory with the passage of time. Thick, old trees became its dense canopy, the sky above vanishing almost completely, with only occasional streaks of sunlight touching the forest floor which was peppered with twisted roots, small stones, and fungi.

Our homes were surrounded by abundant vines intertwined with moss-covered boulders amidst towering trees, on which barks those purple-orange wild orchids thrived.

Crudely-built bamboo gates served as the entrance to our small town, if anyone can find it at all—for we did not want to be found.

In the heart of our village, an idle spring graced the center. Meager underwater life flourished in its shallow part. Around its edges, swamp-like vegetation grew despite the water's olive color caused by algae and swirling mud.

This particular forest's surreal ambiance became a haven for our people, a stark contrast to the hell from which they escaped in the North.

Determined to make a clean break from their former base, my great grandfather enforced his own set of rules among the few who came with him, turning his back on the old, violent ways.

Hard as it was at the beginning, completely different from the way they had been brought up to, he was obeyed and revered nonetheless.

His strict rules proved to be beneficial to our community. It brought long-lasting peace and harmony.

In effect, our tribe ceased to be hunters. Instead, we became economically self-sufficient by planting our own crops as well as poultry farming. We lived very simple lives, preferring to keep to ourselves, hidden from civilization.

The local government, in the few times they unwittingly and unwelcomingly chanced upon us, tried to extend help and support in any way. But we always declined, telling them we were fine on our own.

After all, the children were taught rudimentary reading and writing by their parents. It didn't matter that none of us experienced formal schooling. No one wanted to leave our town, anyway.

This was our home. Like our ancestors, we all knew and accepted that it is here that our remains will be laid to their final rest.

My family's firstborn sons, generation after generation, by virtue of a distinctly inherent trait unique only to our lineage, retained leadership over our little village.

When my father passed away, the torch was rightfully given to me. Malek's advisorial and other important skills remained a permanent fixture, acting as my mentor.

"You should know I would not succumb to a woman's charms to the detriment of our people, Malek."

"Is that right?" He steadily met my gaze.

I felt my temper rising. "I would tread carefully if I were you, Malek. You are bordering on disrespect."

Immediately contrite, he bowed his head. "Forgive me, Datu. But the old folks have come to me with their. . .observations."

The old folks. The ones we addressed as The Elders. Ten old, wrinkled women, they were known to possess wise insight and sharp perception with many years of experience on *things* that the younger generation had not yet encountered. And like Malek, they lived like hermits.

It was peculiar that they took the time to leave the comforts of their dwelling to encourage Malek to speak to me about this.

I asked, more out of curiosity than anything else, "What are they saying?"

"That she's an *encantada*."

I burst out laughing. "Malek, surely, you don't believe such things can exist in our village!"

Unperturbed, he went on, his face expressionless. "There are certain mysteries we cannot explain. An open mind may prove to be a lifesaver. And the Elders feel she is not a white *encantada*, but a black one. The evil kind."

"I do not think so," I argued, my mind already disregarding the outrageous accusation.

"Datu." His voice matched the steel in his eyes. "May I remind you, they are the Elders. You should at least hear them out."

"And why, pray tell, would they think of her like that?" I fumed.

"Other than their instincts? She lives alone in the clinic with her collection of bottles, which contents are suspicious. One child reportedly saw her with a frog in her hands."

I rolled my eyes. "Malek, she's a doctor. And she's not just an ordinary doctor. She's a virologist. She creates vaccines that cure diseases. She has a great sense of duty too.

How many doctors of that kind, much less lady doctors like her, have volunteered to practice their work here in our village? None. The last doctor sent by the government had ulterior motives."

His face darkened at the memory, but only momentarily. Malek was an expert in clamping down emotions.

"Yes, that's what's worrying me. Why isn't she afraid to live and work here, alone? I find it hard to believe that she doesn't know the dangers of being in a remote area such as ours."

"I would think that's why she brought her own radio communication system, Malek. With batteries to boot. She's not a fool."

"What good would that do to her if she's dead?"

"Malek," my voice took on a hard edge.

He knew when to stop. "Forgive me once again, my friend. But I am truly concerned for your welfare as well as for the safety of our people. Nena suits you more."

The mention of my childhood friend whom everyone was expecting me to marry made me seethe.

I replied to him forcefully, "I appreciate your concern. But believe me when I say that I am your ruler and I know what I am doing. I have not lost sight of my duty to my people. I intend to fulfill what my father and his ancestors have done before me."

I remembered the brooding, disbelieving look he gave me that day. Did he know his advice would go unheeded?

CHAPTER 3
The Doctor

The first time I saw her angelic face with her prominent cheekbones and brown doe-like eyes, I was smitten.

Marie came to us one fine summer morning, banging enthusiastically at our bamboo gates. She claimed she had volunteered to practice medicine in our community with the permission of the local government.

Before any of us could refuse, she had set camp, virtually occupying an empty, dilapidated hut. Over the course of the following weeks, she transformed it into a clinic, installing her things, books, and other possessions, despite our angry protests and snide remarks.

While other strangers had cowered and fled from my people's sharp looks and defensive stance, she stood her ground and went on her merry way.

She wasn't scared of us, of being alone deep within the forest with people she didn't know. Maybe it was that courage that earned her our respect.

In time, her cheery disposition and tutoring sessions endeared her quickly to the children. She was untiring in her efforts to teach basic first aid as well as other domestic chores to the women. She charmed even my most stoic, hardened men with her tasteful cooking, proving true the adage that the way to a man's heart is through his stomach.

She was also the first woman who had the guts to stand up to me.

Once, an outbreak of *dengue* fever almost downed all the children. I assured her repeatedly that our people's stamina can overcome it. But she was adamant, haughtily ordering me to purchase bottles of isotonic drink from the nearest town to increase the little ones' depleting platelets, after I flatly rejected her proposition of blood transfusion, an abomination to our culture.

We shouted at each other in front of my people. In the end, she furiously marched away into the night. Come morning, she returned, bringing with her boxes upon boxes of hydrating drinks, making house-to-house rounds, urging the sick children to drink them. In no time at all, little feet were running all over the place again, a stark contrast from the gloom that pervaded the day before.

When I offered to pay her for her purchases, she answered me imperiously. "I don't care about the money. I care for these children. You should, too."

It was the first time I wanted to kiss her breathless, if not for the villager's eyes fearfully watching for my reaction. Instead, I turned my back on her, pretending to be furious.

I realized one other thing that day: *she would make a good mother.*

CHAPTER 4

In Her Eyes

There was this one stormy night. The battering winds were howling so loud, our ears were hurting. Hard rain slammed above us, drenching our roofs. Blinding lightning and powerful thunder were playing hide and seek in the ebony clouds.

She opened her door warily when I knocked. Her large, anxious mocha eyes and quivering red lips were obvious signs of how panic-stricken she was, but she was too proud to admit it.

"What do you want?" she demanded.

At that moment, I almost told her that I wanted so very much to run my fingers through her silky mane. Black as midnight, her wavy hair cascaded behind her back, down to her waist, freed from the confines of a tight braid that was her usual style.

Instead, I smiled down at her and spoke gently, "I want you to read me a story."

"Read a story? In this weather?" she asked incredulously.

"Yes. While sipping a cup of hot coffee, if you don't mind my company."

She thought I was joking. But when I returned her gaze steadily, she let out a sigh of relief and rewarded me with her dimpled smile. She knew I was there for her, that I was telling her she shouldn't be afraid of the storm, or of anything. Because I was there *with* her.

That night, she read me a book by the flickering candlelight. At first, her voice shook, her fright still evident. Eventually, her soft, melodic voice soared above the deafening thunderclaps and beating rain, its rhythm more forceful in its serene strength and tone.

I didn't remember the words, nor the story. But the image of her curled up on the couch, her dainty feet tucked under her legs, her hands reverently holding the book she was reading was what stayed in my mind. She fell asleep with her head leaned back against the couch, book on her lap, her creamy, slender neck gracefully exposed.

Such temptation to my eyes, a blatant offering for me to take.

But with her, I wanted everything to be right.

Only with her.

I covered her gently with a blanket and watched over her as the storm raged on through the night. When the first ray of sunlight peeked from behind the clouds the following morning, I was gone.

She searched for me, thanking me profusely for the night before. From then on, her attitude towards me changed. She grew less wary of me. Gradually, we spent more time together. Slowly, we became friends. And with each passing day, my love for Marie deepened.

We talked a lot about many things. She was a good listener. She would look me in the eyes and listen attentively to what I was saying, making me feel important. I told her what my ancestors wanted for our tribe: peace and prosperity, away from modern society. I told her about my sweet, unassuming mother whom I lost to a devastating storm when I was but a child. I shared stories of how my father, the gentle strongman, raised me single-handedly and prepared me to be a leader of integrity and responsibility.

She, on the other hand, talked mostly of her life as a student of medicine and her work as a doctor, of the thrill of finding cures and culturing organisms. I couldn't understand her enthusiasm for those things, but I didn't mind. I was content with just being with her for almost all my waking hours.

I should have realized that even back then, I knew almost nothing about her personal life, except that she was a childless widow.

I became her shadow. I helped her in the clinic, arranging the bottles filled with chemicals which names I couldn't care less.

She read to the children and I hovered nearby, wagging my finger to anyone who would dare move an inch.

The women giggled as I frustratingly tried to pluck a head of cabbage from its base using my bare hands, a chore I hadn't done in all my years of living—all because she needed it for cooking.

My men shriveled in fright whenever I caught them staring at her for longer than three seconds.

And my heart soared with joy every time I was rewarded by her coy glances and prudent smiles.

I took her to the forest's many mystical, magical spots.

We walked through stony, elevated paths, hand in hand, bringing with us a basket of food and water.

I brought her to my favorite place, a tiny waterfall, where silver liquid poured from a high, rocky mountain edge, falling into rivulets of water puddles that made up the clear, sparkling, shallow brook below it.

She gasped in delight when I took her to a secret garden unknown to man, of wild orchids and wild plants thriving under the umbrella of an ancient tree's vast, extensive web of large branches and leaves.

She clung to me for safety when we climbed up the rough cliff just beyond the village, reaching its peak to view with awe and wonder the magnificent beauty of nature down below.

As the months passed, there were subtle, conspicuous changes that brought me immense pleasure.

Several times, I caught her looking at me with tenderness and would hastily turn away, her cheeks blushing.

She would wear summer dresses that emphasize her femininity, discarding the usual scrub suit of the past.

She wore her hair down, letting me tuck stray locks behind her ear to put a wild orchid there.

And whenever I was playing with the children or talking seriously with my men, or issuing instructions to the women, I would catch her watching me with genuine admiration and shyly flash me her sweet smile.

All these gestures made me hope. But there was only one way I can be sure.

They say the eyes are the windows to the soul, and I believe it to be true.

Each day, I made sure to look into her eyes, getting glimpses of various emotions: wariness, fear, excitement, curiosity, sadness, worry, confidence.

And *anger*. Flashes of hateful anger surfaced from time to time, for which reason I couldn't understand.

Hate and one other emotion: *indecision.* These two intermingled in fleeting instances.

But whenever I started to ask her about it, she would lower her lashes, shutting it down, replacing it with something else again. Like it was never there in the first place.

Patiently, I waited. Until I can see a certain elusive emotion I was searching for in her eyes, I knew she wasn't ready.

Every night, we retired to the clinic and she would read me stories, with me bidding her goodnight afterward.

In the beginning, we were seated facing each other. Gradually, we moved nearer and nearer to one another, until we found ourselves curled up with each other, her head cradled on my neck, my arms around her.

One night, after a year of reading and cuddling, when the moon was full and its moonbeams filtered through the onyx-colored clouds above us, *I kissed her.*

She kissed me back, and the smoldering heat that was our lips consumed us for what seemed like forever. Flustered at her spontaneous reaction, she drew back.

I gazed deep into her eyes and saw them being conflicted.

Yet, as plain as sunlight, I also glimpsed a certain emotion more intense, *an emotion that mirrored mine,* which I had longed for the longest time to see.

Love.

She tried to fight it, but couldn't. When I captured her lips once more, she was lost in turbulent passion, just as I was.

I was so happy that I pushed away the nagging thoughts at the back of my mind.

I ignored the persistent voice that questioned *why,* aside from love, was there still traces of anger in her eyes.

The only thing that mattered at that moment was our lips colliding, both of us surrendering at last to the intense feeling that can no longer be denied, that had been growing and flourishing with each passing day we were together.

I could have taken her that night. I could have made her mine then and there.

But with her, I wanted everything to be right.

Only with her.

We were wed the following week, when the last sun-rays kissed the ground on our feet, when the cold air of the night was beginning to be felt.

I gave her a necklace with a gold locket as a wedding gift.

The Elders performed the wedding ritual according to our customs which she gladly embraced. We sealed our vows with a lingering kiss.

The people dined on sumptuous food and wine all night. There was dancing, vivacious arms waving from side to side above swaying heads, feet stomping firmly to the beat of the joyful rhythm of the drums.

I held her hand throughout the celebration, exchanging smiles as we watched our people.

A few times I caught her smile waning, replaced with a frown, and I tugged at her fingers to get a glimpse of her eyes to know what she was feeling. But her smile always came back, her eyes downcast.

Foolishly, as only someone blindly in love could be, I attributed it to nerves and exhaustion.

From his home, Malek silently watched, vigilant as always.

CHAPTER 5

The Treasure Hunter's Story

D o you want me to tell you a story?" she asked me as I nibbled on her ear, a prelude to our lovemaking.

At last, the celebration was over and the people had retired to their homes, leaving us the privacy I had ached for all night.

"Now? Must you?" In jest, I answered, my breath fanning her neck, rejoicing when she responded with a shiver.

"Yes," her cheeks on fire, she laughingly pushed me away, though her hands lingered on my chest where my heart was beating fast, hungry for her touch. "Listen."

My arms did not budge and my lips did not stop, trailing kisses on her neck. "Go on, I'm listening."

"There was this man who left his wife with the promise to come back with riches far beyond their wildest dreams."

Her voice hitched and she choked out a low moan, as her wedding dress dropped unceremoniously to the floor, my eyes feasting on her naked glory.

But she was determined to finish her story even as she stammered, her body quaking with passion.

"T-the man was g-gone for a long time, and the wife grew worried. Still, she waited and prayed for his safe return. Finally, after five long years, he came back to her. But he was broken and sick and barely alive, dying in her arms the night of his return."

I murmured, "That's a sad story," my lips and hands weaving their own intricate tale of heated frenzy and unrelenting lust on every part of her body.

"What," her breath came out in gasps, her desire matching mine, soaring to heightened proportions, "what do you think the wife did?"

"My darling," I grunted, "right now, I cannot think of any other wife except mine," as I fused our bodies into one, her intoxicating warmth filling me with such glorious pleasure that can only be akin to heaven.

It was the last memory I had before the terror I awakened to.

CHAPTER 6
The Real Story

W-what are you?" I didn't recognize my voice. It was guttural, thick with anguish.

She stood towering before me, a diabolical smile pasted on her face. Where was my wife, Marie, my loving, caring, better half? Who was this stranger with the wild, crazy eyes, holding an empty bottle that I assumed was the home of the black widow spider inside me?

"Revenge." She hissed.

"I don't understand," baffled, my breath came out in gasps. "What did I do to you?"

"Not you. Your father," she replied scathingly.

"My father," I groaned in extreme pain, "is dead."

"Yes. Such a pity. I would have wanted him to suffer as you are suffering now. As you and your entire village are suffering now."

My insides were twisting. Fire, hot and torrid, burned within me. I felt weak and utterly helpless.

"How...how did a black *encantada* like you managed to sneak into us?"

Her laugh was crisp and garish. "I am flattered that you'd think of me that way. But no, I am not a black *encantada* any more than you are a human, Datu," she spat out.

My eyes widened. "Y-you knew, all along?"

"Yes," she jeered. "Thanks to my former husband's sketchy map, I found your secret little tribe of *tikbalangs*."

At her words, my lower body shook vigorously.

Unmasked and freed from pretense, my legs slowly, painfully metamorphosed, turning to disproportionate, aching limbs. Toes folded and closed up, binding into flesh, nails disappearing to become hooves. A black, thick tail jutted out excruciatingly from my behind.

But my arms, torso, and head strangely refused to transform. Undoubtedly, the poisonous black widow was wreaking extreme havoc inside me, preventing my natural form to surface fully.

I, Datu, the proud king of horse demons or *tikbalangs* in this side of the world, laid sprawled on the bed. Disgraced, dishonored, humiliated beyond compare. A dismal, unsightly figure of half-horse, half-human: dangling limbs, hooves, and tail with a disfigured, disintegrating body—and the face of a man still desperately in love with his new bride.

"The story. It was you," I realized.

She spat at me, eyes blazing with hate. "Your father placed a curse on my husband.

He was insane, disoriented, more bones than flesh when he found his way back to me. I lost my husband because of your father!"

I shook my head, correcting her, swallowing hard the acute pain that continually pierced through me.

"You're wrong. It wasn't my father who cursed him. It was Malek, the *Kapre,* our family's guardian since time immemorial."

Blinking rapidly, she frowned in disbelief. "No. You're lying," she breathed.

I snarled, remembering the smooth-tongued, selfish man that had plunged our tiny village into darkness years ago.

"It was your husband who was a liar and a thief! He used his profession as a doctor to come here. We trusted him! But by nightfall of his first week here, he tried to steal Malek's pot of gold, killing his wife and son by plucking out their hearts with his scalpel in their sleep."

She took a step back, her wicked smile slipping from her lips, her face a picture of uncertainty and denial. "No! It can't be. That can't be true!"

"I swear on my father's grave, it is the truth! What your husband suffered was a righteous punishment for his crime. He was lucky my peace-loving father ordered Malek to free him from the curse so he can get back to his family." I swallowed painfully. "To you."

She knew that I, or any of my people, will never use my father's grave on trivial matters. It was against our Laws, punishable by death.

Relics and even memories of past kings were not taken lightly without consequence in our tribe.

Realization and acceptance dawned on her. Her eyes widened. Her face twisted in horror.

"What have I done?" she screeched.

CHAPTER 7
The Perfect Weapon

What did you do to my people, Marie? What is this malady I suffer?"

Haltingly, she confessed. She had poisoned the water, making sure all the women and children drank it at the wedding reception. They were the lucky ones. A painless, merciful death, they will wake no more to another morning.

The men, including me, were another matter. In human medical terms, our condition was known as necrotizing fasciitis, an infection caused by a bacteria that eats flesh. She found a way to culture the *Group A Streptococcus bacteria,* making it a hundred times more potent than the kind suffered by ordinary humans.

Using black widow spiders and other insects as carriers, the deadly bacteria invaded our skin through their punctures while we slept after the feast, eating our skin's protein and connective tissues with tremendous speed and ferocity.

In a day or two, our bodies will deteriorate quickly, our tissues will be fully destroyed, our muscles will totally decay. More blisters, bumps, black dots, and other skin lesions will appear amid the onset of fever, weakness, nausea, and vomiting. Even the most powerful antibiotics would not be able to cure us.

Driven by blind fury and revenge, her genius mind had devised the perfect weapon to annihilate our tribe.

CHAPTER 8
Love, Unmistakably

The sounds of ear-splitting grief and anguish reached my ears, a cacophony of awful, spine-chilling wails and cries mixed with high-pitched, distressed neighs.

The men had found their families dead and had realized their misery. Heavy hooves marched, stomping wildly, the ground shaking with the intensity of an earthquake.

In any minute, they would be arriving, and they will demand Marie's blood.

My human eyes took notice of her face, white and drained of all color. A few moments ago, she had been prepared to die as a consequence of her action.

But now, the realization that she did it for all the wrong reasons caused her to feel unspeakable terror and dread, knowing the horrible death that awaited her.

Death, indeed, was inevitable. There was just one thing I wanted to know.

Had to know, *for everything else depended on it.*

"You loved your first husband so much that you planned and executed this revenge." My chest heaved with a certain heaviness I haven't felt before in my entire life. *"What about me? Did you not love me at all?"*

I held her eyes fixedly to my own, as I waited with bated breath for her reply.

The eyes are the windows to the soul. *And I, as king of the tikbalangs, have the magical power to gaze the truth behind them.*

Those deep swirls of warm honey pools which had bewitched my heart and rendered me captive returned my gaze, sparkling with tears at the edges. Where fury blazed but a few moments ago, in its place I found suffering, guilt, remorse, and... dare I hope?

Love. Yes. *There it was, unmistakably.*

Love poured forth from her eyes, telling me everything I wanted to hear even before she spoke.

"I did. *I do!* But I thought your father. . . Forgive me! I wish I hadn't come here, wish I hadn't done these terrible, terrible things. The children! Petra, Benny, and the others! The

Elders! The women! Datu, my love, forgive me!"

Burying her face in her hands, she wailed like a banshee: gut-wrenching, deafening, harrowing.

It was enough for me.

CHAPTER 9
The Verdict

Malek was the first to arrive, unscathed, as I knew he would be.

Being a thousand-year-old *Kapre,* his skin was tough and callous as metal. No insect can bite into, much more, penetrate it. He was the lucky one.

Behind him, my men, all twenty of them, stood in their full *tikbalang* form. They were a sorry sight to behold.

Some of them were without a limb, a hand, an ear, a nose. I counted three who had open, fresh wounds on their bodies, gory pus flowing profusely. There was one whose face was torn asunder, his skull protruding from a hollow, empty cheek. Still another had only one eye, the other being eaten by a hungry beetle making its way to his brain.

The putrid stench of decaying flesh wafted in our midst, reminiscent of rotten eggs and rancid old cheese.

Like zombies, they snarled and shrieked, hungry for vengeance. Copious tears mingled with blood, sweat, and mucus, an appalling spectacle of a wretched race.

"What has she done to us? To our families?"

"Her life must not be spared! Death to her!"

"Pain, pain all over! We cannot bear this kind of agony!"

Malek growled for them to stop. The silence that followed was heavy. I knew it would not be long. Impatient, angry hooves were shuffling, jerking, ready to punch at any moment, greedy for retribution.

My mentor, my best friend, my guardian, took one look at my mutilated hand, his face grim. I felt, rather than heard, the words 'I told you so.'

Yet, he respectfully bowed his head before me as always, and murmured, "Tell me what I *need* to know, my friend."

Malek needed to know if I have done my *duty*. Over and above all, it was his priority.

I stared at Marie. Cowering in a corner, her eyes were squeezed shut. Her whole body was shaking. Her hands cupped her mouth, stifling her cries.

Awaiting her death sentence.

Turning to Malek, I solemnly nodded. I thought I saw tears spring from his eyes, but it was quickly set aside. He nodded back at me.

He knew what must be done.

His raspy voice boomed loud and clear over us. "She is your queen, and as such, she is untouchable. Our Laws are clear on that."

I heard Marie's soft gasp, surprised and unbelieving.

All hell broke loose as the men screamed expletives, shouting of vengeance. They were all bark and no bite. They knew better than to break our Laws.

When the noise died down, someone was bold enough to demand a solution to the problem at hand.

"What about us? We can't live like this!"

Malek gravely agreed. "I know."

With an earsplitting growl, he sprung at them. In a haze, I saw claws. Fangs. Heads thrown in the air, torn apart from bodies. Blood, a mixture of crimson and black, spurting, gushing, flooding the floor.

In a matter of minutes, it was over. Every one of my men was dead. A humane act, a swift end to their affliction. Death with honor at the hands of our guardian.

Malek did what must be done.

If allowed to live, their condition would force them to be savage beasts, reduced to cannibals, killing each other—the harsh reality from which my great grandfather had escaped from, when a dreadful plague struck our kind a millennium ago.

It was to Malek that the burden of ensuring it would not happen again was entrusted.

It was a vow he took when our family saved him from barbaric humans and took him in.

CHAPTER 10
Legacy

Marie stood aghast, stunned at the murderous rampage which had just occurred.

"I-I don't understand," she muttered, her lips quivering.

Hurriedly, because time was short, I groped at the back of my head, my fingers fumbling, searching.

With a loud roar, I plucked out three gold, thick hairs.

Handing them to her, I urged her, "Put this inside the gold locket I gave you, and wear the necklace at all times. No *tikbalang* will harm you for as long as you live. Then go to the gates and dig the ground underneath it. You will find a pot of gold. It is now yours to keep."

"W-why are you doing this?" tremulously, she whispered.

I smiled wanly. "You know the answer to that, my darling."

Fresh, new set of pearl-shaped tears rolled down her cheeks. She came rushing to me, wailing, unmindful of my ghastly appearance.

She clung to me and I relished her touch. Desperately, I claimed her lips, drowning myself in their sweet, sugary depths.

One last time.

When it was over, I whispered to her ear, "When you leave here, do not look back. Do not return to this forest, for this will be no more. There will be no trace of us, or even of you. Leave now, my darling. And know that I have loved you more than any man had, and ever would."

She nodded, mutely. I shoved her towards the door, and with a last lingering look, she ran, away from the bloodshed, away from the terror, away from me.

My blurry, failing eyes lovingly followed her until I cannot see her anymore.

Exhaling a labored breath, I spoke to Malek, my back to him.

"Give me your word, Malek."

"I will protect her, Datu. Guardian I was to you, and guardian I shall always be, to yours. As I have been to your family before you. *For eternity.*"

"Then. . . I am ready, my friend." I faced him. My best friend, my mentor.

My executioner.

Malek placed his heavy hand on my shoulder. A drop of tear made its way down his blackish brown, deeply-lined face.

Our giant guardian was a sentimental old fool, after all.

"It has been my honor serving you, Datu."

Despite the torturous pain, I managed to smile. "You have served me well, Malek. For that, I am forever grateful."

Without a word, his hand slid down abruptly to my chest. I felt his sharp claws dig in my flesh, clamping down hard and fast, effortlessly burrowing through thick muscles, severing veins, crushing my ribcage. With an anguished groan, he tore my heart out from my chest in one fluid motion.

In a haze, I stared with wonder at my faintly beating heart, raised in the air, nested in Malek's blood-soaked hands.

Before oblivion came, a sense of utter peace descended upon me.

I had lived a full life. I had known how it was to love and be loved.

And I had fulfilled my duty, as my ancestors before me had done.

My seed had been planted.

It would grow and thrive. It would overcome whatever odds may come its way. It would be a *male* that will begin another bloodline.

This, I know, for this was the way it has always been with every *first* seed in our family.

Once, I thought this distinctly inherent trait unique only to our lineage of *original tikbalangs* was a curse. But now, it was nothing short of a blessing.

Our legacy will endure.

My son is safe.

In her womb.

* * * THE END * * *

FILIPINO TERMS USED IN THIS BOOK

Tikbalang

The *tikbalang* has the head of a horse and the body of a human. In Philippine folklore, a *tikbalang* is a shape-shifter that haunts certain places in the wildlands. It dwells in the forests and mountains of the Philippines. In some traditions, *tikbalangs* can change their shape into that of humans and can also become invisible.

Kapre

Kapre may be described as a tree giant, tall (7 to 9 ft), dark-coloured and hairy. It is normally depicted as a docile, tree dwelling, cigar smoking creature.

Encantada

An *encantada* is a fairy, nymph, goddess or enchanted person who is believed to guard natural creations such as forests, seas, mountains, land and air.

ABOUT MAYUMI CRUZ

Mayumi Cruz is an award-winning indie author writing diverse, cross-genre fiction. To date, she has published thirteen books and co-authored four anthologies.

Chroma Hearts, her Psychological Thriller novel, was awarded 2019 Best Published Story of the Year by Penmasters' League where she was also recognized as 3rd Best Published Author.

Some of her writings have also appeared in Philippines Graphic and other online and print publications.

Also an artist, Mayumi holds degrees in Economics and Educational Management.

Her books are available on Amazon and other digital bookstores.

Connect with her at her:

Website: www.mayumi-cruz.com

Facebook:www.facebook.com/MayumiCruzAuthorPage/